Legend Of The
HULA MOOSE

By Christine Taylor Sprowl Tetak
Illustrations by Diane Lucas

Legend Of The Hula Moose

Library of Congress
LCCN: 2009908376

ISBN: 978-0-615-54123-5

You are invited to discover the Legend of the Hula Moose Website at: www.legendofthehulamoose.com

Travel to the Kids Page and have fun with word searches and coloring pages from the original pencil sketches by Diane Lucas.

Published by Hula Moose Farm LLC. P.O. Box 190686, Hawi, HI 96719

Illustrations by Diane Lucas. (www.lucasillustration.com)

Prepress and printed by Imaging Hawaii LLC (www.imaginghawaii.com)

DEDICATION

I wish to dedicate this book to the memory of my father, Walter Hamilton Taylor. He was a retired Santa Monica Fire Department firefighter and former captain with the California State Department of Forestry. While Captain he directed wayward kids in firefighting techniques. He taught me to use my imagination and to laugh.

Walter Hamilton Taylor
Aloha mua loa!

ACKNOWLEDGMENTS

My extreme gratitude is to my husband, Robert Tetak; the real Lopaka. We share a love of the islands, history, culture, people and "aloha spirit" that inspired me to write this book. He listened to this story many times as it evolved, assisting in the research, dialogue and editing.

I also offer my thanks to the Hawaiian Na Hoku award winning slack key guitar music of John Keawe; Peter and Susan Denman for the gift of the Nancy Lamb book, *The Art and Craft of Storytelling*; KohalaBookShop.com for the King Kamehameha books; The Bond Library in Kapa'au for finding the wonderful tiny book, *The Hawaiian Longhorn Story*; Petroglyph Press for reprinting the book and making available the art of John Webber and books by the poet artist Don Blanding.

I want to express my appreciation for the artwork of Diane Lucas. She brings the story to life with her beautiful illustrations. I'm grateful for Yahoo, Wikipedia, and Amazon.com. These sites put me in touch with history and facts I needed to write this historical fiction. I also wish to thank Allison Brown at CreateSpace.com for guiding the story to publication.

CONTENTS

PROLOGUE

You might wonder how two young moose from Canada could end up on a ship bound for the Hawaiian Islands with a herd of longhorn cattle. Well, let's climb aboard Captain Vancouver's ship *HMS Discovery* and take this adventure together!

The story begins as the cold of winter is approaching the coast of British Columbia. The year is 1793.

The king of England commissioned Captain George Vancouver to explore the western coast of North America. His orders were to search for an inland passage connecting the Pacific and Atlantic Oceans while mapping the coastal waterways.

After completing this task the crew was preparing the ship for a return voyage to the Hawaiian Islands, where it is always warm and pleasant.

Captain Vancouver gathered gifts for the Great King Kamehameha (kah-may-ha-may-ha) of Hawai'i Island. He hoped the king would be impressed with a small herd of longhorn cattle purchased from a ranch in British Columbia.

CHAPTER ONE
Friends Flock Together

Two stray yearling moose met after becoming separated from their mothers during winter's first big snow storm. While exploring on their own the moose spotted a herd of longhorn cattle.

"Look at those creatures!" the young male moose bellowed. "What do you think they are?"

"I don't know" the female replied. "I miss my mother! Don't you miss yours?"

"Of course I do!" he exclaimed. "I wonder where she could have gone?" he thought.

Being young and curious they began to mingle with the herd. While enjoying their new friends, they were swept up by Captain Vancouver's inexperienced crew who thought the young moose to be a type of cow. The men rounded up the cattle into a corral. The gate snapped shut behind them!

   The moose were missing their mothers but felt warm and safe with the herd as they huddled together against the freezing winds. The moose had no idea that they were destined to be included as gifts for a king on a far-away island.

CHAPTER TWO
Long Ocean Voyage

The wind howled and heavy snow fell on the morning of their departure. The cattle were carefully escorted onto the ship over a creaking, old wooden ramp. As they entered the lower part of the ship the light flickered and gradually dimmed as the sailors closed the hatch to their new crowded quarters.

The moose worried about what they had gotten themselves into. Their mood improved as they saw fresh water in buckets and hay on the floor.

A few sheep and goats were included on the voyage. All of the animals, especially the cattle were nervous, bellowing and mooing as they settled into the cargo deck of the ship.

Nobody seemed to notice that the moose pair looked different than the cattle. The moose had a dark brown coat of fur like some of their mates and they were about the same size. The female had a little highlight of tan fur around her eyes. The same shaggy fur was on her mane and continued over the small hump on the back of her neck. The male had soft and friendly eyes with a furry hanging clump shaped like a bell on the underside of his throat. His moose antlers, still undeveloped were just little bumps on the sides of his head.

The ship was a busy, noisy and stinky place. Below deck was a symphony of animal sounds. The moose quietly observed everything around them. Although anxious and frightened about the mysterious adventure unfolding, there was no turning back now!

Every morning and evening Walaka, (wah-law-kah) an old Hawaiian man with a gray beard came down the ladder to feed the animals. He was born on Hawai'i Island; spoke English and Hawaiian, acting as interpreter for Captain Vancouver.

Walaka had an important job caring for the animals that were gifts for his king. He brought fresh water, cured hay and grains for the hungry animals.

The sheep and goats remained calm, but the cattle became quite difficult. They hated the cramped quarters, constant rocking of the ship and were always restless. Whatever Walaka did to please them would not change their grumpy attitude.

It was Walaka who first noticed the pair of moose.

"You're a strange looking pair" he spoke to the moose in a soft, reassuring voice. "Looks like you were in the wrong place at the wrong time!"

The old man liked that the moose were part of the herd. He didn't see any reason to report their presence. Walaka named the stowaways after his parents Lopaka (low-paw-kah) and Keena.

10

CHAPTER THREE
The Cattle Landing

After a long voyage through rough seas and storms, the ship finally reached Hawaii Island. It arrived at Kawaihae (kah-why-hi) harbor on the northwest coast of the island. The animals were weak from the voyage with the frailest brought to shore in the chief's large canoes.

Thousands of curious Hawaiians were drawn to view the cattle landing. The natives had never seen cattle and were terrified of the large wild beasts. They called the animals "wild hogs."

The moose and cattle were excited to be on land again. They kicked up their heels on the beach while the frightened islanders climbed the coconut trees for safety or plunged into the sea to escape the ferocious beasts.

12

CHAPTER FOUR
The Wild Moose Escape

After the chaos of the landing, the animals were herded to a large lava rock corral located near the harbor. The perils of the two-thousand mile voyage had taken a toll. The dangerously thin cattle needed to fatten up and recover before presentation to the king.

The men moved the herd slowly by the Great Stone Temple on Whale Hill. It was a war temple built by Kamehameha and thousands of his men. The heiau (hay-ow) was constructed using lava rocks hand carried twenty miles from Pololu (poh-low-lu) Valley at the northern tip of the island.

Suddenly the sky turned dark and a lightning bolt flashed illuminating the clouds, followed by a loud clap of thunder that shook the ground. Heavy rain began to fall, drenching the animals and the men as they were trying to drive the unruly herd. Frightened, the animals began to stampede, running past the temple, over the rocky hills and toward the mountain.

"Run for those mountains Keena!" Lopaka shouted. "This is our chance to get away!"

Lopaka and Keena raced past the slower cattle leaving them behind. A few of the bulls caught up with them after reaching a stream where they stopped to rest. The group continued climbing up the foothills toward the massive volcano Mauna Loa. The men chased the remaining cattle into a gully uphill from the harbor, managing to capture most of the herd.

The cooler climate on the mountain and the snow on the peak reminded Lopaka and Keena of their home in Canada. The storm passed, the rain stopped and a rainbow arched across the sky.

CHAPTER FIVE
The Celebration and The Royal Kapu

Captain Vancouver was not happy about the loss of animals in the stampede. He sent his best men to search on foot for the rest of the missing cattle. They found a few strays that were too weak to move, put a rope around their necks and led them back to the corral.

After a few weeks, the animals regained their strength. They were fit and ready to be presented to the king.

There was a great celebration with hula dancing and a huge feast. Food was wrapped in banana leaves, placed on red hot coals in a pit covered with dirt and cooked for hours. The menu included fresh pounded poi (poy), fish, roasted pig, bananas, and breadfruit. It was a joyful occasion!

16

The king was pleased with his gifts. Captain Vancouver encouraged him to protect the cattle. Kamehameha ordered a royal kapu that it was forbidden to harm them for twenty years. He wanted the herds to flourish and grow.

After the feast, the king with Captain Vancouver by his side released the bulls and cows to roam the island.

The herd gathered behind a big bull leading them to the lush, green pasture land of Waimea valley. After their release the island landscape was never the same again.

CHAPTER SIX
A Different Look

As time went by Lopaka began to develop strange-looking horns coming out the sides of his head. These horns were not like the long pointed ones of their friends the longhorns, but flatter and wider with scalloped edges. Lopaka was growing his first set of moose antlers!

The moose had legs and faces much longer than the cows with a large shaggy hump on the back of their necks. Unlike the cows, they ate bark, twigs and branches from the trees.

Noticing the changes in the moose, the cattle became distant and drifted away leaving them on their own. Lopaka and Keena were sad to lose their friends.

Occasionally they saw the cattle at the stream where they liked to gather. Keena had a favorite cow friend. Her name was Peke (pay-kay) and she was brown with a little white streak on her nose. They would play in the stream and graze together. Then her loyal friend would disappear back to the herd.

20

CHAPTER SEVEN
New Island Friends

While exploring the island, Lopaka and Keena made some new friends. First they met a Pueo, (poo-ay-oh) a graceful owl with bright yellow eyes that hunts during the day. This bird liked to swoop over their heads, hover and then land in the 'Ohi'a trees towering over them. This became a daily event.

There were other birds, the 'Apapane (ah- paw-paw-nay) dressed in crimson reds and the gray-brown 'Oma'o (oh-mah-o) that sang in sweet whistled and flute-like notes each morning and every evening.

The beauty of the island with its morning rain, colorful rainbows, abundant food and fresh water was beyond anything the moose had ever dreamed!

CHAPTER EIGHT
Mauna Loa Erupts!

One day the moose were playing on the snowy peak of Mauna Loa. They stopped and noticed the mountain-top glowing red. Their faces felt hot as they looked at the black sky. The air became thick with smoke making their eyes water and breathing difficult. They sensed the danger and knew they must escape!

"I'm frightened Lopaka" Keena cried. "I can't see through this smoke and my eyes burn!"

"Follow the whistles of our friends the birds Keena" he replied. "They're leading us in the right direction!"

They were afraid but their new friends, the tropical birds, helped lead them swiftly down the mountain to a safe place on the island.

During their escape they ran into a large group of wild boars or pua'a (poo-ah-ah). The pigs had short legs, dark coarse hair, and long snouts with dangerous tusks on both sides of their powerful jaws.

The boars made loud grunting sounds as they dug and grubbed into the earth for tasty morsels of roots and bugs. This also frightened the young moose and they quickly galloped around the busy pigs.

Their retreat took them past cascading waterfalls as they left the forest behind, finally arriving safely at the beach. It was a welcome change from the volcano's molten lava and belching smoke.

They saw ferns, fragrant flowers and swaying palm trees full of coconuts. The coolness of the wet sand refreshed their sore hooves. The air was warmer than what they enjoyed on the mountain, but with each breath, the sweet smell of the ocean air lifted their spirits.

CHAPTER NINE
The Green Sea Turtle

One evening under a full moon, Lopaka and Keena were frolicking along the beach darting in and out of the crashing waves. Off in the distance they noticed a green sea turtle. The honu meant business digging a nesting hole in the sand with her hind flippers. Sand was flying all around; drops of tears rolled down leathery cheeks, cleaning sand from the turtle's eyes.

They watched her through a thicket of ironwood trees, trying not to disturb this fascinating shelled beach creature.

The turtle laid her eggs dropping them one at a time into a carefully crafted nest. With skill and urgency she covered her eggs with damp sand, slowly crawling away. She labored

awkwardly, dragging her heavy body across the sand. She stopped on the lava rocks near the ocean's edge.

Finally, the moose politely approached her. She said, "My name is Melia." Now she was ready to "talk story."

"It has been twenty years since I left this island to explore the ocean. I've been nearly eaten by hungry tiger sharks and almost crushed in the tentacles of a giant squid. I narrowly escaped drowning when caught in a fishing net laid to harvest tuna. It is a miracle that I survived and was able to return to the island where I was born."

The moose listened intently, captivated by her story.

It had been a long ocean journey, one flipper stroke at a time and she was feeling a little weak from laying over one hundred eggs. After telling her story, she wanted a moment of calm and quiet before entering the sea.

28

CHAPTER TEN
Paniolo (pah-knee-oh-lo)
The Hawaiian Cowboys

After Mauna Loa stopped erupting, Lopaka and Keena returned from the beach. The moose were glad the forest had avoided much of the devastation from the lava flows. They thrived munching on the meadow grasses and browsing on shrubs. Twigs and bark were still abundant from the majestic Koa and 'Ohi'a (o-he-ah) trees on the great volcanic mountain.

Their favorite hideaway to visit was a pond below a waterfall. They spent many days at this cool, refreshing place.

One time the moose were knee-deep in the pond when they were startled by a strange sound. They stood very still, frozen for a moment. The hair on their back humps stood straight up.

Their ears lay back when they heard horses galloping and human voices.

Horses and cowboys were new to the island. They were from California, invited by King Kamehameha to teach the Hawaiians how to handle the wild cattle herds. The paniolo rode the cow ponies using a special Hawaiian saddle with a raw-hide lariat to rope and capture cattle.

The cowboys stopped suddenly when they caught a glimpse of the moose. Lopaka and Keena retreated quickly, disappearing into the forest.

It was getting late in the day and the sunset was breathtaking in bright pinks, purples and oranges. The cowboys had little time to wonder about their sighting. Night was approaching and they needed to drive the stray cattle back to the ranch before darkness fell.

Soon after arriving back at the ranch, they told the other paniolo at dinner about seeing moose near the mountain-top. The cowboys chuckled with disbelief at the amazing story. They laughed it off, thinking the story a joke or just an imaginary tale.

Throughout the years there were more sightings, usually rejected by most as a fable.

These stories spawned the Legend of the Hula Moose. However, anyone with good sense knew that there were no moose in Hawai'i!

CHAPTER ELEVEN
Growing Family
The Legend Continues!

Lopaka and Keena settled in the upland mountains of the island. There were cool hidden valleys, waterfall ponds, and rainforests with plenty of food for grazing and browsing. During the winter they could even play in the snow!

Their family grew through the years, yet they were rarely seen by the Hawaiian people. The few who did catch a glimpse of them thought they looked like strange cattle. Rumors persisted---and the Legend of the Hula Moose grew a life of its own!

EPILOGUE
Can You See the Hula Moose?

Some people say that the moose are just a legend and that mystical rainbows over Mauna Loa enchanted the Hawaiian people into believing they had actually seen them.

To this day if you are driving on Saddle Road near Mauna Loa at the edge of the forest and a rainbow appears with the sun at just the right angle, perhaps you might see the Hula Moose browsing or playing in the snow on their adopted Hawai'i Island home.

PAU (POW)
THE END

AFTERWORD

I am a first grade teacher who has read thousands of beautiful stories to the children in my classes. After many trips to Hawai'i Island, I became inspired by the history, culture and "aloha spirit" to write *Legend of the Hula Moose*. I wish to thank my students at Guadalupe Elementary School (Union School District) in San Jose, California for being the first audience for this book.

This story demonstrates that living creatures can adjust to unfamiliar surroundings, make new friends, and overcome all obstacles to thrive. The moose are helped in their adaptation to island life by the other animals, illustrating that everybody, including moose, needs love and guidance to achieve success.

ALOHA!

GLOSSARY OF TERMS

Aloha mua loa With love forever

ʻApapane (ah-paw-paw-nay) Native Hawaiian bird

Breadfruit Round green fruits the size of a cantaloupe.

Browsing When moose browse they are searching for food choices to eat such as twigs, shrubs, bark and leaves. While browsing they can reach up to ten feet above the ground.

George Vancouver British naval captain and explorer who visited the islands several times between 1792 and 1794 and was a friend to King Kamehameha

Honu (hoe-new) Hawaiian green sea turtle

Ironwood Tree An evergreen tree, native to Australia, that resembles a pine tree

Kapu (kah-poo) A taboo; something forbidden.

Kawaihae Harbor (kah-why-hi) Port of entry for sea vessels on the northwest Kohala coast of Hawai'i Hawaiian meaning: Water of Wrath

King Kamehameha (1758-1819) (kay-may-ha-may-ha) The warrior king of Hawai'i. He became king in 1792 and united the islands in 1810.

Kilikina (Keena) Christine

Koa Tall majestic tree native to the Hawaiian Islands.

Lava Extremely hot melted rock erupting from a volcano.

Lopaka (low-paw-kah) Robert

Mauna Loa Largest volcano on earth in terms of area covered and one of five volcanoes that form Hawaii Island It is an active volcano.

Melia (mah-lee-ah) Plumeria flower

Molten Reduced to liquid by heat; melted.

'Ohi'a (oh-he-ah) Large rain-forest tree native to the Hawaiian Islands

'Oma'o (oh-maw-oh) Dark gray-brown singing bird native to Hawaii Island

Paniolo Hawaiian cowboy. They learned their (paw-knee-oh-low) craft from Californian and Mexican vaqueros. The word in *espanol* was hawaiianized into paniolo.

Pau (pow) The End

Peke (pay-kay) Betty

Poi (poy) Paste made from the taro root. It is the main item on the Hawaiian menu. It is eaten with fingers.

Pololu Valley A deep valley with cliffs in North Kohala. King Kamehameha lived there as a small child.

Pua'a (poo-ah-ah) Hawaiian pig/wild boar

Pueo (poo-ay-oh) A Hawaiian owl revered as a guardian spirit by the ancient Hawaiians.

Pu'ukohola Heiau (poo-oo-ko-hoe-lah) Temple on Whale Hill. Built by King Kamehameha for his war god. (hay-ow)

Talk story Term used by Hawaiians when telling a story; making conversation.

Walaka (wah-law-kah) Walter